CW00918864

HORROR
HIGH
AND
The Interghouls Cricket Cup

Random House Australia Pty Ltd
20 Alfred Street, Milsons Point NSW 2061
http://www.randomhouse.com.au

Sydney New York Toronto
London Auckland Johannesburg

First published by Random House Australia 2005

National Library of Australia
Cataloguing-in-Publication Entry

Stafford, Paul, 1966–.
The interghouls cricket cup.

For children aged 9–14 years.
ISBN 1 74166 045 9.

I. Title. (Series: Horror high; 2).

A823.3

Cover illustration and design by Douglas Holgate
Internal illustrations by Douglas Holgate
Typeset by Midland Typesetters, Australia
Printed and bound by Griffin Press, Netley, South Australia

10 9 8 7 6 5 4 3 2 1

AND

The Interghouls Cricket Cup

Paul Stafford

RANDOM HOUSE AUSTRALIA

The Rollcall

'I'm warning you, all of you! This absenteeism will cease or I promise you a slow, ugly death by dot-to-dot disembowelment, followed by some really serious consequences.'

The Rollcall Master was addressing the back wall where the dried, curled-up scalps of a dozen former pupils were nailed randomly like a collection of used Odor-Eaters, but the class knew he was watching them through evil eyes in the back of his head.

Mr Grimsweather was fully cranked in his rant at the class, snarling in top gear, virtually sweating blood. 'Dire consequences! Hell to pay! I'll go straight to the School Execution Committee; see if I won't. Absentees from rollcall better have an exceedingly good excuse or it's the long drop for them – double death, slow and hideous, then fast and horrible. Am I making myself crystal clear?'

The class sat statue still, completely silent. The dusty human skeleton hanging lifeless on the wall next to the classroom door looked ready to nod its scaly skull in solemn assent. Since its skull had a metre-long sharpened steel spike hammered right through one ear and out the other, it'd be a pretty cool trick if it could pull it off.

'I'm making myself crystal clear, right?' persisted Grimsweather. 'Right. Now, one final time – Jason-Jock Werewolf, are you here?'

There was a long, long pause before Geoff Dandyline opened his mouth. He just couldn't help himself.

Grimsweather instantly shot him a malevolent glare. 'Yes, Dandyline?'

'Nothing, sir.'

'You opened your mouth to say something fabulously stupid, Dandyline. What were you going to say?'

Dandyline adamantly shook his head, self-consciously rubbing his latest shocking fatal neck wound. 'Nothing, sir. Honest, sir. Just drying my teeth, sir.'

'And?' said Grimsweather.

'And now they're dry, sir – very nice. Only, I was wondering, like, since you mentioned exceedingly good excuses, I was wondering, like, well, what's an exceedingly good excuse exactly? Sir.'

'Why, Dandyline?' snapped Grimsweather. 'Have you got one for that brainless head of yours?'

'Oh no, sir. I mean yes, sir. I mean . . .'

'No, Dandyline, I'm mean – mean as marmoset measles, especially when you get me started, so don't. An exceedingly good excuse for being absent might be a funeral, a reincarnation or a dead-raising. I'd accept coma, car wreck, exorcism, bomb blast, gas explosion, multiple homicide and nasty-painful-death-at-the-hands-of-a-mean-evil-deadly-serious-how's-your-father?-my-dad's-great-I-will-KILL-YOU-serial killer. And maybe flu, if you've got a doctor's certificate. Nothing else. Why do you ask, Dandyline?'

Dandyline shifted in his seat and crossed his legs and dug his fingernails into the palms of his hands and concentrated and really tried, but just couldn't quite prevent his trademark dumb grin straddling his face like a ferret riding a bush buffalo. His buckteeth danced out of his mouth like a conga line of chalky skeletons.

'Well, Dandyline?' pressed Grimsweather.

'Quite well, thank you, sir,' replied Dandyline brightly. 'Apart from this neck wound which is kinda itchy and festy, but thanks for asking, sir.'

'I wasn't asking, curse you! Last chance, Dandyline. Where is Jason-Jock Werewolf and why are you grinning?'

'I'm not grinning, sir,' Dandyline shrugged, grinning. Then he grinned again, only more inanely than usual. 'I'm just wondering if cricket practice is an exceedingly good excuse, sir?'

'Cricket practice? Cricket practice . . .' Grimsweather repeated the word as though tasting it on the tip of his decrepit, black tongue. 'Cricket practice. Hmm . . . yes, I think I'd accept that one. Why, Dandyline?'

'Because Jason-Jock is practising with the Werewolves XI team for the Interghouls Cricket Cup, sir. They've never won it, sir, they're desperate, practising twenty-seven hours a day, nine days a week. And while we're on the subject of sport, sir, I'll be absent tomorrow practising head bowling. Sir.'

'Head bowling? What the devil is head bowling?'

'It's tenpin bowling using one's own head, sir.' Dandyline gaped so enthusiastically his horse-teeth fanned out like a bunch of freshly peeled bananas. 'I'm in the regional finals.'

'What sort of excuse is that?' Grimsweather snorted. 'What sort of sport is that? Head bowling! Do you take me for a complete fool, Dandyline?'

'A complete fool, sir? No, sir – sort of half-finished.'

'Guillotine, Dandyline. Lunchtime. You know the place.'

'No, sir! Please, sir! Each chop shaves a slice off my neck and I'm too young to shave, sir. Please, sir, my neck's out of slices, I've no neck left – I look like a bullfrog, sir.'

Grimsweather nearly smiled, for the first time ever. 'You should be grateful, Dandyline – that's a vast improvement.'

The Lesson

Chapter 1

The trouble started (as it often does in low-carb, fossil-fuelled stories like this) with a bug-house bet between inebriated school principals, a skeleton crushed into powder and blended into some tripped-out hippy health shake (and understandably irate about it), and a naive, adolescent werewolf who believed the solutions to his insurmountable personal problems lay in a book.

Solutions in a book? Bah. No wonder the dude had problems . . .

Anyway, the trouble really started when Jason-Jock Werewolf took stinky advice from a brain-dead, head case bystander, listened to it and then actually acted on it. The advice was offered by one of those cheapo, project-kit Frankensteins you see loitering around public places trying to look like someone who has a clue, and JJ was fooled. Should've changed his name to Jason-Jock Jackass.

Listen. Don't ever take advice. Wrong-headed people the world over will try to give you guidance when things get ropey, pretending they've been in that exact situation, navigated their way safely through it and learnt grand and prudent lessons, but their advice is always dangerously defective.

Unless the words of wisdom have come from some officially registered and internationally recognised source of deep wisdom – such as myself – ignore them. That's my advice.

For example, Jason-Jock Werewolf was

misguidedly advised that the key to overcoming his many nefarious problems, dilemmas and general weirdnesses was to get actively involved in a team sport, such as cricket.

Yet the insurmountable problems haunting Jason-Jock only intensified as the red six-stitcher cricket ball now whizzed past his bat and crashed through his stumps.

'Howzat?!'

JJ groaned as he gazed back at the stumps. They had been in a pleasing and precisely upright arrangement – three stumps supporting two bails, all tickety-boo and how-do-you-do – just seconds ago. Now they'd spun out all over the place like a madman's chopsticks, middle stump flat on its back, bails a metre away in the dirt.

'You're out,' shouted the coach. 'Again. For a duck . . . again. Quack, quack, quack. Back to the pavilion – next batsman.'

Jason-Jock shook his head in deep despair. So far today he'd been out nine times for a total score of zero, nine ducks in a row, enough to open a duck farm and sell the eggs for a living. He was the team captain and its best batsman, so you can imagine what the worst ones scored – do the maths, it'll hurt your brain.

The other young werewolves crouching in cricket whites on the pavilion benches bowed their heads, muttering darkly while picking at stray fleas. They were doomed and they knew it. And not just doomed as a cricket team either – their future at Horror High was over. They were going to be expelled unless, unless . . .

Unless they pulled off the impossible.

Anybody who knows werewolves will tell you they can be extremely capable creatures when they put their minds to it. They have the heightened senses of a dog, the supernatural abilities of a ghoul, and the never-say-die spirit of a human who thinks there's nothing peculiar in shedding a quarter kilo of hair on your lounge every time they come to your house to watch the greyhound races on TV.

All of which means they can pull out some pretty gnarly and difficult stuff when pressed. The 'unlikely' they could do easily, being werewolves, and the 'doubtful' was pretty much a walk in the park without a leash. The 'improbable' was imminently achievable, and even incompetent werewolves could pull off 'no-chance' type gigs standing on their hairy heads.

But the 'impossible'? As the term 'impossible' suggests, that was impossible, even for someone as cool and righteous as myself, which these werewolves definitely weren't.

And what Principal Skullwater demanded – winning the Interghouls Cricket Cup – was fully and totally and thoroughly impossible. Yet if they didn't pull it off the werewolves were out of Horror High.

Expelled. Evicted. Banished. Exorcised. Forever . . .

Chapter 2

Principal Skullwater had observed the werewolf cricket team practising in the nets over the last months and been the sorry witness to their inter-class matches these last miserable weeks.

They were rubbish.

Skullwater lived and breathed cricket, but at 2305 years of age he found running between the wickets a little beyond him. Still, he followed cricket avidly and made foolhardy, ill-advised and ridiculously ambitious bets on the outcome of certain matches.

One of these dimbulbous bets had been with Principal Nettlebottom of Death Valley High, concerning the outcome of this year's Interghouls Cricket Cup.

The two principals had argued and bickered on the subject during the annual principals' conference. Nettlebottom reckoned he had an unbeatable team of vampire cricketers at Death Valley High this year. He ranted and raved about them, never letting up for a minute. He got in Skullwater's scabrous old ear for hours, boasting and bragging long and loud on this theme, and surreptitiously filling and refilling Skullwater's glass with strong whisky.

Pretty soon the combination of whisky and braggy drove Skullwater to the point of no return, and he slurringly made a very dumb bet using the kind of snaggle-toothed language all principals use when they're completely trolleyed on strong liquors.

It wasn't until Skullwater returned pie-eyed to school and slowly recovered from the cracking aftermath that he realised just how dreadful Horror High's werewolf cricket team was, and just how very dumb his corresponding bet had been. He was in deep trouble.

Trouble? He was cactus.

Now the principal was really starting to agonise over it. Was this evidence of the gypsy curse returning? Was it a sign it was back, the relentless curse that had blighted his third life back in Roman Britain, then thoroughly soiled his eighth life in the Middle Ages? The curse that returned twice as strong in his eleventh life, forcing him to spend most of his days in the court of Vlad the Impaler, dressed in a clown suit and jumping through hoops like some retarded circus goat?

The same curse had cost him his chance at the presidency of the Oddfellows' Society in 1756 and recurred again in the 1930s when all his valuable shares in handkerchief futures crashed during the Great Depression. You'd think during a great depression that hankies would be at an excellent price, everybody depressed and dejected and moping on down.

You'd think.

But that's where the curse bit deepest – it turned everything normal abnormal, everything downsideup to upsidedown.

It wasn't the first time Skullwater wished he had refrained from snickering and hooting out loud when that 93-year-old gypsy woman fell headlong into a stinky overflowing latrine, back in the days of the Roman occupation of ancient London. But considering the circumstances, who wouldn't laugh?

He wouldn't, that's who. Not now, knowing what he knew.

The ancient gypsy crone had cursed him five ways to Fingleton, and it was a quality curse that followed Skullwater throughout his many unhappy lives, sticking to him like a stink sticks to baboons.

They sure didn't make blights like that anymore, and now it appeared Skullwater's long-wearing, all-weather, frequent-flier-points curse was back. He hadn't cured himself of it last time round like he'd hoped, even with a humungous dose of antibiotics.

The mere memory of that mordant and mortifying medication made Skullwater wince. The antibiotics gave him the runs like the fudge falls in Willy Wonka's factory, a wicked rash 'round the rude regions, and a head as seedy and degenerate looking as a pineapple plucked lengthways out the wrong end of a rhinoceros.

But it didn't shift the curse one inch . . .

Chapter 3

Of all the foolish things to wager, Principal Skullwater and Principal Nettlebottom had bet their schools' latest acquisitions – the rare, valuable and totally essential portable classrooms each school had just received from the Department of Education After Death.

D.E.A.D. was notoriously tight with money and Horror schools were rarely granted the extra portable classrooms they so sorely required. Both schools were bursting at the seams and these portable classrooms represented the only chance the schools had to adequately house their overflow of students.

Right now extra classes at Horror High were being conducted under trees, in stormwater drains, in the bus shelter and under a tatty white canopy constructed from two enormous pairs of Y-fronts stolen off a rock troll's clothesline and stitched together with wire. None of these solutions was anywhere near ideal, though the Y-fronts doubled up nicely as a spare movie screen for the school's ratty old film projector.

Now the parents of Horror were up in arms, and not just about the stolen undies.

Just like any normal society, the community of the undead wanted to raise their children with higher expectations and better access to education than they'd had. They paid their taxes and figured the least the government could do was provide a decent school system for their ungrateful, delinquent kids, so they could learn their times tables and how to spell rite before they finally ended up in juvie.

That's what parents wanted and they might as well have asked for a cherry on top, too, because D.E.A.D. was not in the business of pleasing parents or schools. They figured the schools could look after themselves since there were plenty of Y-fronts hanging on plenty of clotheslines just begging to be stolen, with the added advantage that rock trolls can't chase thieves further than twenty steps.

But this was also an election year and the Horror Council had to somehow make it look like they cared about educating the young undead, and protect their phoney-baloney jobs. They had a meeting to discuss how they could successfully con the voters this time around.

With the crucial election looming, and every likelihood that voters were not going to be satisfied with thunderbags-related solutions, the council bit the silver bullet and spent some serious money for a change.

Both schools were granted portable classrooms, and they were pretty flash, too – reverse-cycle aircon, double-glazed windows, online computers, broadband streaming, the works. They even had their own toilet blocks stuck on their rear, just where you'd expect to find a toilet.

The bean counters at D.E.A.D. made it explicitly clear to each principal – this generous gift was definitely a one-off. The schools had sod all chance of getting another one of these huge-o, expenso, portable classrooms before the next Ice Age, and since the next Ice Age in Horror wasn't due until the same year Hitler's lawyers got him past the pearly gates and into Heaven, the schools had better look after them.

So you see the predicament. If Horror High lost the Interghouls Cricket Cup and Skullwater lost his whisky-inspired bet, the school lost its portable classroom.

And if that happened Horror High was severely overstocked with students, with no room to house them. Some students would have to go, and since it was the crappy cricketing werewolves' fault, guess who was out?

Not too hard to guess, even for you . . .

Principal Skullwater summoned Jason-Jock to his office shortly after his realisation Horror High would surely and definitely lose the Interghouls Cricket Cup and his bet and the school's lovely new portable classroom.

Obviously Skullwater couldn't reveal the details of the dodgy bet, but felt duty bound to warn Jason-Jock what was in store for him and his hairy brethren should they be defeated in the high-stakes match.

Jason-Jock knocked on the heavy wooden door of the principal's office.

'Come in,' barked Skullwater.

The nervous young werewolf pushed through the door and sniffed the air apprehensively. Something was wrong. 'You wanted to see me, sir?'

'Ah yes, young Mr Werewolf. Have a seat.'

Jason-Jock sat, resisting the urge to scratch at a flea outbreak in his left armpit.

Skullwater straightened his tatty black funeral tie. He had to break the news gently, subtly, with all the caring compassion that modern undead principals are renowned for. 'Now . . . yes. If you werewolves don't win the Interghouls Cricket Cup, you're out on your useless furry butts. There, that wasn't so difficult.'

'What?!' yelped Jason-Jock. 'Why?'

'Well, it's like this, and here's the absolute, deadset, straight truth. As principal of Horror High it's up to me to make the tough decisions – students understand that and love me for it. And it's been drawn to my attention that we're dangerously short on space at this school due to an alarming increase in monsterism. Things are tough all over, so we're going to have to lose some students. It's not my fault – honest. It's all because of the D.E.A.D.

'They've done some market research

out in the Horror community to determine what people expect from a modern undead school. They hired a team of hack pollsters to gauge the community's attitude and the results they came back with are interesting and startling to say the least. It seems the good citizens of Horror expect to see ghosts, goblins, mummies and vampires in our schools, maybe even the odd Yeti, Yowie or foreign exchange ghoul, but nobody actually mentioned werewolves.'

Skullwater shook his head, feigning sadness. 'Problem is, people just don't regard werewolves as an essential feature of a modern, balanced community school. Fact is, and here's the gospel truth – strike me dead if I'm lying – they consider werewolves more animal than human and more suited to the dog pound than a school. Add to this the fact that werewolves don't do anything very useful and take up valuable classroom space.'

Jason-Jock was in shock. He didn't know what to say, so Skullwater kept going.

This lie was getting easier and easier to tell the thicker the principal laid it on.

'See, here's the skinny on our students, according to the community; ghosts are fine, they don't take up any space at all and we could cram a million into a milk jug. Goblins are useful since they double as garden gnomes. Mummies are pretty much indispensable – they're handy for extra bandages in case of accidents and extra loo paper in case of emergencies and anyway, everybody loves their mummie. And the vampires keep the sick bay's blood bank stocked up, of course. But what, I ask you, do werewolves do?'

Jason-Jock was still in shock, but he stirred in his seat enough to crank an answer out of his numb skull. 'We keep the feral cats away,' he offered.

'Feral cats?' drooled Skullwater. 'I like feral cats. In fact I love feral cat, roasted with garlic and served with a spicy mint jelly. No, Mr Werewolf, you'll have to do better than that. Far as I can tell, a werewolf is just a fat kid having a bad hair day, so you'll get no quarter from me. Here's the deal – if you werewolves can start pulling your weight and proving yourself indispensable to the school, you can stay. If your cricket team can win the Interghouls Cricket Cup and demonstrate yourselves to be useful after all, you can remain at Horror High. You win – you stay. You lose – you stray. Now get out there in the nets and practise.'

And that was that.

Chapter 4

Jason-Jock tried explaining the situation to the pack of werewolves flocking nervously around him. They milled about in stunned silence, trying to absorb the news. Nobody spoke.

When somebody did speak it'd have to be Fleabag O'Brian, the least qualified among them to have even a half-baked opinion. Nevertheless Fleabag opened his elongated jaw first. He looked like he was about to cry.

'Cripes. We'll all end up living back at the pound. I hate the pound. All those stinky kids patting puppies, all those vets administering rabies shots, all those overflowing litter trays. All those nasty kittens . . .'

Jason-Jock shook his hairy head. 'No way. We're not going to the pound. We've got to win the Cup.'

Howls of derision and helplessness rose from the pack.

'Win?' yelped Howler Binks. 'We'll never win.' Howler was a fourth-rate batsman, very silly mid-on fielder and general hubbub spokesman of the conference. 'We're useless – and I'm the optimist of the team.'

Jason-Jock wasn't to be discouraged. 'Okay, I admit we're not much good – yet. But we haven't got a choice. If we give up now, we're kicked out of school. If we lose the Cup, we're kicked out. Either way it's the same result. Or we could try like we've never tried before.'

The others agreed with the noble sentiment, but what were they to do?

'Okay,' said JJ, 'here's the plan.

Fleabag, go borrow all the cricket DVDs you can find at the video store – we're going to study all the famous games of the past. Howler, you hit the library, same deal – get all the cricket books you can find, anything you think might be useful.

'Chomper, go through the sports shed for cricket equipment – we need to get our hands on some decent gear for a change; "borrow" some. Grubby, you take the video camera and secretly get some footage of the opposition teams so we've some idea of what we're up against.'

'Okay,' replied Grubby. 'But what are you going to do?'

Jason-Jock smiled mysteriously. 'I'm going to consult my secret weapon . . .'

Jason-Jock's secret weapon was a book. A book? Phooey. You were hoping it'd be a light sabre or a set of magic boxing gloves or at least an Uzi with the serial number filed off. Get real – where would a teenage werewolf get his paws on an Uzi? You need a licence for one of those.

No, it was only a book, but a very special book, or so JJ thought. He believed every little thing that was written in it, the dense fool. It had been sold to him by an out-of-work bookseller posing as an out-of-work magician who was actually an out-of-work scientist.

Scientists are not to be trusted – fact. It's got nothing to do with their goofy appearance, though that thing your mother said about always judging a book by its cover is certainly true in this case.

The fact that scientists have Coke bottle glasses, ears like the sails of a blue-water racing yacht and a flipped-out afro like Hair Bear has got to tell you something's not right. They hide behind their nerd screen but can't resist using their big brains for evil rather than good.

In this case, the scientist who duped Jason-Jock had a great need of money. His mobile phone had been cancelled for non-payment of bills, and he owed his mum for accidental overpayment of pocket money.

Not even the fried chicken place would take his cheques anymore.

Cash was what he needed and he didn't mind how he got it. The villain sat down and wrote the biggest pile of spuriously spoony hogwash possible, published it and sold it to Jason-Jock from his dodgy book-store, claiming it was a magic book.

The book, *Everyday Magik By a Magician Who Knows*, was supposed to be a deeply powerful magic source, when it was actually just a deeply powerful hoax. The scientist was a common fraudster, like they all are.

How do I know so much about scientists? Let me tell you, I've been through the wringer with those charlatans. I was once approached by scientists to take part in a paid experiment, living in a share apartment for a month with a tame chimpanzee. The scientists wanted to observe the interaction between a civilised being and a backward primate.

I behaved brilliantly and was fully blameless but the whole ordeal was disastrous and embarrassing.

The chimp had obviously been brought up in a bad neighbourhood and its sense of values was whack. It wouldn't do its share of the cooking or cleaning, hogged the remote control, made long-distance phone calls to the deep jungle that it had no intention of ever paying for, took hours in the bathroom, used my special medicated dandruff shampoo and mocked me mercilessly whenever I wet the bed.

After a month of this nonsense I was happy to be rid of the troublesome ape and collect my fee. Then I found out I wasn't the one being paid – the chimp was!

To add insult to injury it turns up on *Oprah* and fully bags me out to the hooting audience, laying it on so thick about me wetting the bed that Oprah nearly wet herself. In order to not get laughed at by complete strangers, I had to wear a fake moustache and curly red wig for the next three years.

Don't talk to me about scientists.

But Jason-Jock was gullible enough to think the crap magic book was real magic truth and followed its directions, instructions and hoaxy spells to the letter. He didn't know about scientists, or maybe he was just soft in the head.

He ran his clawed paws down the contents page and found the chapter titled 'Winning at Cricket'. He read the instructions and smiled to himself wolfishly, as werewolves often do.

Now they'd be okay. Now he knew how to win the Cup. Now their future at Horror High was assured. Now he'd be a hero . . .

Hero. Zero. Dero. All pretty similarly spelt. Guess which term best describes this bozo . . .

Chapter 5

Jason-Jock called a secret meeting of the cricket team in his tree house. The players arrived in dribs and drabs, climbing up the rickety ladder and crawling onto the tree house platform, panting like old steam locomotives.

It would've been a bit convenient if JJ hadn't built his tree house sixty-seven metres up the backyard gum tree, but he'd read a real estate book (probably written by the same sneak scientist) that claimed the top five factors in selecting quality real estate were privacy, a good view and location, location, location. Jason-Jock didn't have any choice on the location, since he had to build his tree house in the oldies' backyard, so he went a bit nuts on the remaining two factors.

Howler was first to arrive. He was always punctual and hated time wasters. He reckoned nothing worth doing should ever take much time and, since he was never batting at the crease for very long, he'd never suffered the embarrassment of publicly disproving his own theory.

Fleabag was next, panting like a resuscitation dummy. He always had a scared, hunted look on his hairy face, and his cricket whites were always freshly laundered. He was packing it now, terrified of heights. The rest of the team often wondered about the connection between Fleabag's many fears and his always washed pants. They wondered, but no amount of curiosity would drive them to investigate further.

Fleabag had no teeth – his baby teeth had fallen out and his adult teeth never came through – and his fur fell out in chunks, due to an unknown allergy. He was a nervous pup, pretty much afraid of everything you could name – postmen, kittens, the wind, country music CDs, nursery rhymes, photos of himself, ice-cream, kites, cakes with pink icing.

He couldn't howl either.

Grubby came next, a tougher kind of werewolf but a heaps scungy and festy sort of dude. Nobody wanted to sit next to Grubby on the benches. At any one time he could be harbouring nits, fleas, lice, ringworm, cattle ticks, jock rot, northside mange and crack rash, and that was *after* he'd been dragged through a chemical bath. He was well-regarded by the team, but even he acknowledged he was a walking, talking body bag of deadly infectious diseases.

Fangbert was the next to arrive and after Jason-Jock he was the best cricketer. He had the longest fangs of all the werewolves and was kinda vain about them. He cleaned them three times a day, flossed and buffed them, and polished them up with that showbiz oil weightlifters lube their muscles with. He was also pretty cool and the chicks dug him, which irritated the other werewolves no end. They pretended they didn't care and were only interested in cricket, but they all knew if a girl gave them a second look they'd give cricket the flick faster than J-Lo ditching her freshest husband.

Whitetail, Steppenwolf, Clawpaw and Dingus arrived in a group, having stopped along the way to polish off some road kill. They were growing lads, always hungry, always eating, but not always carrying enough pocket money to stop off at the Horror mall for a burger or falafel. Enough said.

Chomper came last. He was always late. Pretty soon he was going to wish he'd never come at all . . .

Jason-Jock called the meeting to order.

'Right, you guys. I've been consulting my book of magic and I think I've come up with a spell to help us win. It's not a very pleasant spell but I don't see that we have any choice. We've practised and practised, and if there's been any change in our form at all it's that we've got worse. I'm not suggesting we admit defeat and cheat, but as your captain I suggest we admit defeat and cheat. That's my advice.'

What did I tell you about taking advice?

The other werewolves glanced at each other and shrugged. Werewolves don't have any particularly strong feelings about cheating, one way or the other. People ignorantly assume that because they're related to dogs they're some kind of noble beast, with strong morals. Let me tell you, there are month-old leftovers festering away in your skanky long intestine that have more moral fibre than your average werewolf, and living in that biodegradable slop are microscopic critters much less inclined to cheat in order to win a cricket match.

When Jason-Jock mentioned cheating, he wasn't talking about some simple plan like replacing the oppositions' equipment with hollow bats and exploding cricket balls, or burning their eyes with laser beams from a safe distance, or even having them buried in a nest of flesh-eating ants. That would have been lightweight compared to what he had in mind.

No, Jason-Jock's plan was plain wrong, which makes sense since it was lifted word-for-word out of the wrongest kind of wronged-up magic book. And since I don't want to be associated with the plan in any way, I'll let him fill you in on the details . . .

'Our problem is we lack skill. Somehow, someway, we've got to acquire skill. The easiest way? To get the skill from someone else, someone good, someone who is acknowledged as a cricket expert.'

The other werewolves looked blank, though Dingus smiled faintly because he was thinking about food – a rotten cat buried in the neighbour's backyard that his mates didn't know about.

Jason-Jock misguidedly took this as a sign they were clinging to his every word. 'According to my book – which is a genuine magic book, the last in existence in the world – there's only one true and definite guaranteed way to absorb the skill of another player, and that's to literally absorb the player. How do we do that? We dig up the skeleton of a famous cricketer, grind up the bones, mix it with fresh rain-water and drink it. And if we locate a really great dead player, the stuff we drink makes us really great too.'

The other werewolves pulled faces; Fleabag looked terrified; and only Grubby didn't seem too put off. 'Sounds okay – if it works.'

'It'll work,' Jason-Jock assured them. 'I told you – I got it out of this boss magic book, the only one left in the world. Now the big question is, where do we find a great dead player?'

'Easy,' said Fangbert. 'We'll get Warney. He's the best bowler in the world, and a pretty cred middle-order batsman, too.'

'Idiot,' snapped Howler. 'Shane Warne's not dead.'

'Oh, yeah,' replied Fangbert, temporarily downcast but then cheering up fast. 'We could kill him,' he suggested brightly.

'We're not killing anybody,' replied Jason-Jock. 'Not this week. We need somebody already dead.'

But Fangbert wouldn't let up. Shane Warne was his fave player; he idolised him. 'If Warney's still smoking cigarettes, it won't be long before he dies. We could send him a couple of cartons and wait 'til he keels over.'

'Shut up, Fangbert,' snapped Howler. 'We can't wait, and anyway, he's not worth waiting for. He's not that good.'

'He is too!' shouted Fangbert, and leapt to his feet, warm for some form, shaping up for a brawl.

'Heel!' shouted Jason-Jock. 'Sit down now! We're not fighting over this. I'm the captain. I make the decisions and I've already found a suitable skeleton – a perfect specimen. It belonged to WG Grace, a great all-rounder, best player of the 19th century, captain of the English team for twelve years. He's our man.'

'But where's he buried?' asked Fleabag nervously. 'It can't be too far away – I can't travel on trains or buses because the noise scares me, and car trips give me night-mares.'

Jason-Jock shook his head. 'He died in Horror on his last world tour and is buried right here in Horror cemetery. We go for his bones tonight.'

Chapter 6

A world-class cricketer buried in Horror? I have to tell you I find that kind of coincidence exceedingly difficult to swallow, like a single dung beetle employed to deal with the contents of King Kong's toilet pan after he's attended the week-long Prune & Bran Eaters' Conference.

I said as much to the publisher. As coincidences go, I told them, this is simply too much. World class cricketer, best in the history of the game, travels extensively playing all across the globe in hundreds of countries, thousands of different cities and towns, just happens to die right there in Horror and gets dropped in the ground almost in these dudes' backyard?

Yeah right.

There are some seriously far-out coincidences occurring throughout history, but this coincidence . . .

Let's just say it's stretching it, like claiming Michael Jackson is a real boy and not a Pinocchio puppet with a cork nose, or that Ozzie Osbourne's undies once belonged to Albert Einstein and could calculate pi to 600 decimal points while still providing superior hosiery support.

I told the publisher: too much coincidence. Way too much. Unbelievable. Inconceivable. In-your-dreamsable. My readers won't tolerate it, I said – they're not total idiots.

I lied about that bit.

Did the publisher care? Did they listen to my exceptional arguments? According to their research, the intelligence quotient of readers who stoop to this type of literary silage is in the same percentile bracket as a bucket of mullet, with the gullibility of the Tooth Fairy and a brain-bone as thick and impenetrable as an armour-plated, all-terrain vehicle.

Those were the publisher's words, not mine. And as answers go, that one was good enough for me. In fact, I have to admit I quite liked it and will be using it myself in the future.

So we'll move right along . . .

Most kids are put off by graveyards at midnight, but Team Werewolf was made of sterner stuff. Okay, Fleabag wasn't – he stayed at home, whimpering and wussing it up under his doona because a bee was crawling around outside his window – but the others weren't expecting him to turn up and didn't let Fleabag's absence bother them too much.

Anyway, there were enough of them to do the job; three on picks, three on shovels and four more to stand around slacking off like a genuine road crew, pretending to keep watch. From a distance it would certainly have looked like a shady operation – a bunch of shifty looking teenagers, up to no good late at night, lurking in the shadows of a deserted cemetery. You never saw a group of hounds look more guilty about digging up bones.

Luckily no neighbourhood-watching, night-walking do-gooder was out that way to chase the boys off like common mutts, and with the ground wet from recent rain, the workers were able to shift six feet of soil in record time.

After an hour's hard digging they struck the top of the coffin with a hollow thud. The coffin was too heavy to lift free of the grave, so they angled crowbars in under the lip and jimmied the lid off with a dry crack of splitting timber.

And there, dully reflecting the light of the moon, lay the mouldering skeleton of WG Grace, the finest cricketer of his day. His bones were bleached white with age and his bony left hand rested on a dusty old willow cricket bat.

Jason-Jock lowered himself carefully down into the damp, dark hole. When he'd found his footing on the crumbly sides of the fresh opened grave, he reached into the musty coffin and prised up the skull, gingerly passing it up to Grubby.

The disease-ridden, idiot werewolf took the skull in his left paw and the jawbone in his right and, fitting the two together, started making it chatter, 'I'm WG Grace and I'm gonna give you a cricket lesson you'll never forget!' he growled out the corner of his mouth.

'Shut up, clown!' barked Jason-Jock, but behind his back the other werewolves smirked.

I told you they had no common decency.

JJ passed up two collar bones, followed by arm bones, leg bones, short bones, long bones and a weird-looking pelvic bone that some tripped-out hippy could've made into an excellent wind chime for their veranda.

The bones were dropped unceremoniously into a mouldy, old hessian sack, clacking against each other like giant pencils.

Then JJ picked up the ancient cricket bat, thinking it may contain some good cricket magic, too, but the old thing busted into pieces and he tossed it back in the box. The werewolf cricket captain replaced the lid and scrambled out; they shovelled the soil back in place, slapped each other excitedly on the back and scarpered into the night, howling at the solemn old moon.

Chapter 7

Next day the team met back at the tree house where they'd stored the pilfered bones overnight. Jason-Jock had borrowed his mum's coffee grinder, and now the werewolves set to reducing the six foot skeleton to a bag of dust.

I've had some crapulent jobs in my time – including writing no-hoper stories for fat-witted teenagers who wouldn't know a . . . hang on, that's this job – but not even I would've accepted a prospect as totally incorrect as the one facing the werewolves now.

There was no easy way around it. First they had to smash the bones into pieces with a masonry hammer and feed those bits into the coffee grinder. The bones were brittle but it still took hours, and the resulting bone dust came out mixed with coffee grounds, a curious combo of grey and brown – like nothing you're likely to find on the menu board at Starbucks anytime soon. It smelt of desecration and deep dodginess.

Dodginess? According to my spellcheck that word doesn't exist, and it sure doesn't even begin to describe how the evil concoction smelt dry, let alone how it smelt after the bilious brew was infused with water. It was a powdered death shake that even Grubby baulked at.

But drink it they must and drink it they did. One by one, sip for sip, each of the werewolves slowly slurped the sickening slop. To absorb the dead cricketer's skill, they had to absorb this dead cricketer swill, and if that's cheating buy me a ticket on the next bus home.

Finally, after an hour of gagging and half-barfing gulps, it was gone. Chomper glared at Jason-Jock after the last dregs drained out of his cup.

'That's the single most disgusting thing I've ever done. This had better work.'

What happened next all depends on your definition of the term 'work'. It 'worked' on the eleven young werewolves in a most spectacular, volatile and uncompromising manner, causing four days of projectile vomiting, stomach cramps, rampant nausea and explosive buckshot diarrhoea.

They missed three important class tests, a heaps fun school Mufti Day (including a teacher-pupil lung transplant swap) and a vicious schoolyard fist-fight between an ADHD mummie and a cross-eyed imp.

In terms of inheriting WG Grace's superb cricketing skills, the 'magic' brew gave the werewolves runs, but not the sort of runs they were hoping for, between wickets after whacking a cricket ball.

The other werewolves were understandably annoyed at Jason-Jock and his rubbish magic book. But, as if they hadn't suffered enough, the worst was yet to come.

WG Grace might have been an exceedingly talented cricketer, but he was also an exceedingly bad-tempered old geezer. Despite being dead nearly 100 years, the fieriness of his temper had not diminished one jot. Now his bones had been disturbed, his skeleton smashed to bits, ground to dust and drunk by a pack of hooligan werewolves. And his favourite cricket bat was busted.

Now – surprise, surprise – he wanted revenge.

Chapter 8

The first the young werewolves knew about the hellbroth of trouble brewing was the day after they'd recovered from the poisoning. They were meeting in the tree house, Chomper had just arrived – late as usual – and the team was discussing their options for future life, mulling over what they'd do once they were kicked out of school.

Grubby was going to volunteer for medical experiments. Howler was thinking he might join a sledge team and race around the Arctic Circle. Fleabag reckoned he might train as an attack dog, and they all laughed at that despite the depressing baseline theme of the topic. Imagine Fleabag as an attack dog, terrified of everything from laughing clowns to kittens.

And imagine being kicked out of Horror High. They didn't have to imagine it anymore. Now it was going to happen, sure as.

During a lull in the lugubrious conversation they heard the ladder scraping against the tree house platform, shaking and juddering and jigging, swaying under the weight of someone slowly climbing up. But who was this? The whole team was present.

A head appeared, grey hair, parted dead in the middle and severely combed down, old-fashioned style. Then a forehead like an ancient tree trunk, deeply lined, and down the lower branches two eyebrows like cockatoos' nests that held glaring black eyes instead of eggs. Then a bulbous red vein-shot nose and a massive bushy beard covering a crazy angry mouth. The mouth was panting, fighting for breath. 'Why . . . the . . . dickens . . . did you . . . build this . . . blasted thing . . . so blanking high . . .'

'Who are you,' asked Jason-Jock, 'and what are you doing in my tree house?'

With interview skills like that, JJ clearly had a future on *A Current Affair*.

The old bloke dragged himself up onto the platform and glared poisonously at the team. He was slumped on all fours, hyperventilating, trying to catch his breath.

Finally he hissed, 'I'm WG Grace and I'm here to teach you a lesson you'll never forget!'

It took a long time and a stack of pleadings, wheedlings, excusings and super suck-up entreaties to prevent the 19th-century cricketer from following his original plan of grinding the 21st-century werewolves' bones to dust, as a fitting revenge for desecrating his grave and dishonouring his memory.

It was Jason-Jock who finally convinced the angry old coot to forgive them.

He briefed – if 'briefed' means begging on your hands and knees, crying like a little girl – WG Grace on their dastardly dilemma; how, if they lost the cricket match they'd be expelled from school; how they were sure to lose since they were useless; how they'd dug his bones up because they'd identified him as the finest cricketer ever.

The fuming ghost smiled grudgingly at this, nodded with humility and stroked his stonking great eiderdown beard. 'Yes, it were true,' he muttered.

Nineteenth-century ghosts are suckers for flattery, a fact worth remembering if you're ever in a tight spot with the Dead.

This ghost was mondo vain about two things: his undisputed cricketing prowess and his heaps chunky beard. It looked like a shimmering waterfall of grey hair pouring out his mouth, tumbling all the way down his shirtfront into his trousers and fanning out into rippling runnels as it slopped into his strides.

He was scarily hairily.

Jason-Jock had already complimented WG's undisputed cricketing prowess, so when the werewolf cricket captain informed the England cricket captain that Principal Skullwater had targeted the werewolves because they were hairy, WG Grace's mind was galvanised.

WG was so hairy that, if reduced to a mathematical equation for purposes of assessment, he'd have been classified ten per cent human, ninety per cent hair.

One hundred and thirty years ago he'd been the butt of everyone's jolly jokes, the prey of every smart alec with a hokey hair harangue. In a period of history when baldness had been all the fashion for men, women, children and even small dogs, WG had been heinously harassed for his hirsute handicap. A modern day fancy-pants sports psychiatrist would've classified him as a certified victim of hairism and sued someone for heaps.

WG had hoped that'd all changed in the passage of a century of enlightened thinking. How wrong he was and how mad that made him. He frothed at the mouth to hear that in these supposedly tolerant times hair was still such a divisive issue.

He'd hoped society would've evolved and matured in the 90 years he'd been lying in a hole, but he was sadly mistaken. Hippies had come and gone, and now young men with terminal hair issues suffered big-style for their preposterous pelts, their manic manes, their tremulous tresses, their furry fleeces, their creditable curls.

And if WG had spent more time studying his thesaurus instead of combing his absurd shag pile, he could've added a whole bunch more clever and alliterative hair references. He couldn't be bothered (I couldn't either) and now the opportunity has passed forever.

But that's not the point. The point was this: WG Grace had copped all the hairist jokes in his day, and been called everything from 'bear hair' to 'mammoth head' to 'werewolf'. Yes, he'd been called 'werewolf', as though it was an insult, and that was the thing that tipped the scale in our hero's favour.

He felt obvious empathy for Jason-Jock and the werewolf team, and at that moment of weakness he decided to help them.

Sucker!

Chapter 9

Or maybe they were the suckers. God, did WG Grace work those lazy werewolves. Day after day in the nets – batting, bowling, discussions, lectures, more batting and bowling. Panting laps around the oval, push-ups, star-jumps, more batting and bowling.

They studied footage of their opponents while WG pointed out their weak spots, advising them how to capitalise on these areas. They watched DVDs of the real pros, the Aussie team. WG laughed at their girly coloured suits festooned with junk food advertisements and mocked Warney's sissy boy-band haircut and lay-around-the-house lardiness.

Fangbert threw his drink in WG's face and the cricket legend ghost chased the werewolf around the oval, swinging a cricket bat, howling with rage and vowing to crack Fangbert's worthless skull like a rotten emu egg.

But all in all the team got it together, and began to actually play like a team. Then, after three weeks of this tedium, dreariness, monotony and mind-numbingly boring training antics that I won't even begin to burden you with, the legendary competition commenced.

The Interghouls Cricket Cup is, as everybody knows, *the* event of the sporting calendar for ghoul schools. Sure, everybody pretends that the swimming carnival and the hockey play-offs and the rugby are just as prestigious, but these are the same single-celled simpletons who tell you it's not important whether you win or lose but how you play the game.

And we all know which vegetable patch these weeds are growing in – and why instead of being treated as heroes they're treated with herbicide – so let's say no more about it. Winning was everything and every student in every ghoul school knew it. They would've gladly died a second time to win the Cup, and the facts speak for themselves.

Death stalked the Cup. Rates of parental homicide went through the roof this time of year, and psychotically angry parents who knocked off their child for losing the Cup were always let off by the courts on the grounds of justifiable homicide. They were given a pat on the back, an excellent meal in the courthouse cafe at the city's expense, and free parking and carwash vouchers for their next court appearance.

The Interghouls Cricket Cup is a sudden death play-off, as you'd expect from a ghoul school competition. What you might not have expected was that the Werewolves XI, suddenly and impossibly playing tight as any team can play, scorched their more docile opponents, stomped them to Hell and back, winning round after round.

Their skill – and luck – held, and after six matches they found themselves in the finals, pitted against the team that had convincingly held the Cup seven years running, Death Valley High's Vampires XI.

Chapter 10

You might've noticed that clever sleight-of-hand tactic at the end of the last chapter. It's a pretty convenient way of covering a whole lot of story in a very few sentences, and since I'm paid by the page I can legally pad half this story with out-of-date stock market columns and copyright-expired strip cartoons and still come away with the same pay cheque.

Pretty sweet hook-up, eh?

You probably think it's your right to be provided with every comical, quirky detail about the werewolves and their high-jinx cricket antics, since that's what the book's back cover advertised and what the publisher is paying me for. I can respect that. I think you're right. Really.

What I can't do is linger around here until April Fool's Day to hold a mirror up so you can swap notes with the Fool of the Year. Maybe we can arrange for an autograph and get ourselves back to the story, if you don't mind.

You may glare down your nose at these unworthy tactics, since it means you're denied all the nitty-gritty details and noteworthy incidents of those previous six matches against the likes of the Skulls XI and the Savage Cannibals X (who ate their eleventh team-mate for lunch). But why bother sharing pointless stuff like Howler setting the umpire's breeches on fire by accident, trying to light a skyrocket; or Dingus spiking the opposition's drink bucket with laxatives then accidentally drinking four tumblers himself; or Fleabag, running scared, toppling headlong into a garbage can full of snapping turtles that were meant to be the raffle prize.

You don't need to know about the match accidentally scheduled on National Nude Day where both sides, the umpire and the spectators all participated in the raw – an AO episode.

You wouldn't be interested in the match that fell during International Elvis Week, when everyone turned up in big hair, garish glitter suits and 20kg of extra lard strapped to their butts, mumbling 'Thank you very much' and 'This one's for my momma' every time they hit the ball.

And if you persist on the complete low-down on these mangy werewolves and their six long gone but celebrated cricket matches, if you absolutely demand complete documentation and the entire transcript, here's a piece of advice for you – why don't you apply for my job and I'll take yours. I'm sure I'm up to it. Can't be too difficult being a juvenile delinquent . . .

***

The Vampires XI were so confident of year-after-year victory they'd taken to drinking human blood out of the ornate silver cup, permanently staining it a rank, murky purple.

Now, as their teams met on the field of final conflict, they hissed murderously at the werewolves. These bloodsuckers were definitely open for business.

Fleabag whimpered, looked like he'd wet his pants, but Jason-Jock said, 'Don't worry. Be cool.'

That was easy to say, but JJ was worried and far from cool. Things had started bad and rapidly got worse. They lost the toss and the vampires elected to bat, making the most of the lack of light.

Say what? Lack of light? You read it right. See, those villainous vampires got to the head of the cricket committee, sucking on his neck until the owner agreed to reschedule the final match for twelve hours later than usual, ensuring the first ball was bowled at midnight rather than the standard midday.

Midnight, on a nearly moonless night, meant perfect conditions for vampires but disastrously shabby and problematic ones for werewolves.

Vampires have superb night vision, thanks to their finely tuned bat radar that operates much better than eyesight, whereas werewolves have fairly poor eyesight at the best of times, even in broad daylight. At night they were blind and all they had was their powerful sense of smell, which mostly emanated from their cricket shoes.

Because it was midnight and pitch black – the cricket ground had coincidentally forgotten to pay its electricity bill and the night lights had been cut off – the werewolf players were unable to observe the audience or even the stands. And obviously the audience saw nowt, and all chanted for a ticket refund. The werewolves heard the chants and muffled singing, then clearly over the top of it WG Grace shouting, 'Come on boys – let's show them how to play real cricket!'

The team honed in on the sound of

WG's voice and found him sitting alone in the dark stand. These sad excuses for cricketers crowded around, complaining about the murky conditions, telling him they were sure to be beaten and that they might as well give up now.

WG looked disgusted. 'Bah. Listen to you lot, whimpering like a pack of wet dogs. You think this is dark? You should have tried playing cricket from my point of view. You see this . . .' He held his great curtain of face fuzz up in front of their snouts. 'This is like playing at midnight even on the brightest day.

'This great beard blanket was tossed over my head every time I hit the ball, but did it put me off or slow me down? Never! You complain about the lack of light; well, light never penetrated this harness of hair, but it never stopped me. You know why? Because I played from here,' he said, tapping his heart, 'not here,' tapping his eyes. 'So don't give me that cheap whining. Get out there and take them down!'

That was the sort of rousing talk that

appealed to aspirational young werewolves, who are prone to cheap, tub-thumpingly patriotic speeches even more than they're prone to high-pitched whistles. They scurried onto the field of conquest, all fired up once more, brimming with newly stoked confidence.

WG sat back down in his seat and chuckled to himself. Little did the werewolves know, he'd always had his beard and hair done up in ribbons like a girl, not only keeping the hair out of his eyes during play but also helping him get in touch with his feminine side. Sometimes he even played in his maiden aunt's silk knickerbockers. In fact he was wearing them now. Who said being a captain meant sacrificing comfort?

What those hounds didn't know wouldn't hurt them . . .

Chapter 11

The vampires, having won the toss, elected to bat first. Not wanting to tire his best bowlers out too early, Jason-Jock sent Dingus and Steppenwolf to bowl the first few overs.

It was called strategy.

The vampire opening batsmen savaged the ball like Fat Albert at an all-you-can-eat buffet. The batsmen demolished each ball in turn, ate them alive, hammered them flat, cracking the bowlers all over the park.

So much for strategy.

Eight sixes in a row meant that pretty soon the opening batsmen had amassed a half century between them. Pretty soon? Criminy – the game had barely started. Not knowing what else to do, Jason-Jock sent Fangbert in to bowl.

It was a masterstroke. Fangbert, obsessive as always about Warney, had been practising the famous 'Flipper' ball night and day for months. Those bloodsuckers couldn't handle the flipper – they began to fall like ninepins. Within two deliveries he'd dismissed the troublesome opening batsmen, then took the next vampire two balls later.

Then, just for kicks, Fangbert started in on the remaining middle-order vampires with Warney's famous 'Wrong-un'. Wrong-un was right – the result was wrong. The remaining vampires – in their haste to get out of the crease and back to the safety of the pavilion – nearly busted their boilers.

Four overs later they were all out for seventy-seven.

None of this meant the werewolves were out of the doghouse yet. The vampires might have been talented batsmen, like Terry 'Type-O' Taggart and Deadman Walken, but they were truly evil bowlers.

The head vampire opened play from the southern end of the ground with a blistering pace attack that claimed Howler first ball for a duck, smashing his wicket like toothpicks and scorching his new cricket bat so badly it smoked like an extinguished safety match the whole long trip back to the pavilion.

The crowd went mad!

That was first ball. Second ball was launched to Grubby after a seventy-five metre run-up. And I do mean 'launched', like the space shuttle-type launch. The delivery resembled a fiery meteorite more than a cricket ball – head height, deadly accurate. Grubby screeched and, sweating with fear, ducked for cover. Speaking of ducks, next ball took out Grubby's middle stump, but not before snapping his bat clean in half.

Third ball, third victim. Chomper for a duck.

Jeez Louise.

Three out for nowt.

The middle-order werewolves pretty much followed the same pattern, folding like cheap suits. So much for WG's great words of wisdom; in the inky darkness the batsmen simply couldn't see the ball.

Then, in an over-the-top attempt to cow the opposition, gross them out and give them the heebie-jeebies, the vampire bowler drooled blood from his fangs all over the cricket ball.

Bad mistake. In the failing light the vampire's radar had been a distinct advantage, but with the blood-dripping ball now broadcasting a distinctive and powerful scent, the werewolves' superior powers of smell took over.

Now they smelt the ball as it scorched towards them at top speed and lashed out with the bat to great effect. Suddenly runs started amassing from the werewolves' bats. The middle-order batsmen held on for half a dozen overs, slowly stealing runs.

But even with this improved performance, the vampires still seemed to have it all over the werewolves. Every time the wolves clobbered the ball in a big hit, even as it rose over the fielders' heads and looked certain to be sailing for a six, a vampire fielder would transform into a bat and fly up to encase the ball like a black, leathery baseball mitt. It was mighty frustrating to see, and that was just for me watching through night-vision goggles from the stands . . .

Jason-Jock had deliberately put himself second last in the order of batsmen, saving himself in case of emergency – another threadbare stab at strategy. The wickets slowly but inexorably fell and now, finally, he took the crease, to do or die.

The other werewolves had done their best, but now it was up to Captain Jason-Jock

Werewolf and the famous Fleabag, their lamest batsman at the opposite crease, whimpering like a half-toilet-trained kid who's just let off and followed through.

'Suffer!' hissed the vampire captain. 'Suffer, and die!'

'It'll take more than you've got to achieve that,' replied JJ.

The vicious vampire grinned an oily grin. 'Time for re-education, dog.'

'Time for resuscitation, bat.'

The two protagonists looked set to lock horns – not easy between a dog and a bat – when the umpire stepped in. 'Simmer down, boys,' he commanded. 'It's only a game.'

Only a game?

They needed over thirty runs to win. I need an aspirin.

Thirty runs? Not in this lifetime, maestro . . .

The vampires figured these last batsmen must be pretty puny and left their lesser bowlers to deal with them while crowding up close in the fielding positions.

Bad mistake. Jason-Jock cracked their first ball, sending it humming for six. Next ball went hurtling to the boundary for four. The fielders crowded in even closer. One vampire was so close JJ could smell his blood-flavoured chewing gum.

A wild bowl, then a no-ball, but JJ didn't know that and took two steps up the pitch and cracked it, aiming for the boundary. Maybe he was aiming for six, but he hit the fielder at silly mid-on, knocking his head silly mid-off, and the bloody missile flew through the air, hitting the 'Hit Me!' sign on the full and leaving a thick, bloody smear down the middle of the billboard.

Jason-Jock ran around jumping with joy, thinking he'd won himself a car for hitting the coveted sign, as was the long-standing tradition in cricket. It wasn't until the umpire's cry of 'No Ball!' that the werewolf captain noticed the headless vampire through the darkness, slumped beside the pitch.

No ball?

No head!

Chapter 12

Jason-Jock smacked the next ball through the slips for a crafty single, and finally Fleabag was facing his first ball.

Fleabag was always scared to some fair degree but now he was peaking out. The whole team's future rested on his hairy head, and between the captain and himself they had to get another fifteen runs. He wasn't sure he could do it.

Fleabag had been scared stiff of the cricket ball until WG Grace came along. He and WG had practised heaps with a soft red Nerf ball, and soon Fleabag overcame his fear – of Nerf balls.

And that Nerf ball had been bowled by Fleabag's everlovin' coach, an elderly gent with a funny, flappy beard, and both gent and beard had been dead nearly 100 years.

Now Fleabag had to face a killer pace attack with a real, rock-hard ball, launched by an angry, beardless vampire who was his sworn enemy and a paid-up member of the Werewolf Wasters. Fleabag whimpered and his face crinkled up like an overstuffed taco.

He was about to cry.

Jason-Jock met Fleabag halfway up the pitch and patted him on the shoulder. 'Don't panic, Fleabag. What's the worst that can happen?'

'I could be killed!' wailed Fleabag.

'You're a werewolf! You can only be killed by a silver bullet – not a red ball.'

'I could be severely maimed,' Fleabag countered.

'Well,' replied Jason-Jock, 'I'll take my chances with that. You'll be alright. Just try to block the ball and give me the strike. Just don't get out. I'll do the rest.'

'Easier said than done,' replied Fleabag, gritting his teeth and facing up to the bowler.

First ball he faced was an evil in-swinger that literally shaved the bails and left them rocking in the dark. Had the slightest breeze blown, the whole show would've been all over Red Rover, call your aunt who lives in Dover.

Second ball was a yorker that luckily wasn't on stump, or it would've spelt death, D.E.T.H.

Third ball Fleabag played a blocking shot. It worked. Cripes, he thought – I'm not that bad. Which was a lie, but we'll let it go. Everybody needs a dream, even werewolves.

Considering what a monumental wuss he was, Fleabag did really well. Admittedly he was very lucky, closing his eyes and poking his bat out mostly, but he didn't get out.

If there hadn't been so much at stake, Jason-Jock would've been enjoying himself. He cracked the ball to the boundary a couple of times and nearly hit another six, causing the vampire cheer squad to hiss and fizz with savage rage and exhibit symptoms of a broad spectrum of anger management issues.

JJ slipped as he played a cut shot and ran a snappy single, nearly getting himself run out, but finally they were level score with the vampires, and one run away from victory.

Trouble was, Fleabag was the batsman on strike. Could he hold out for one more run? Could he save the day, salvage their chances, rekindle their lives?

Oh, the tension. Oh, the humanity. Oh, my haemorrhoids.

The vampires sent their nastiest bowler in, desperate to uproot Fleabag. The vampire's speciality bowl was dead-bodyline, and his even specialer specialty was slinging deliveries straight into the batsman's head. Now he slowly paced out his run-up, a full 200 metres, 200 steps, so far back he was starting from the ladies' queues at the members' toilets, in a neighbouring stadium.

Fleabag, meantime, was laying down skidmarks in his cricket whites that not even a full bore exorcism would ever remove.

The run-up began, slowly, gathering pace. Flecks of blood sprayed from the bowler's murderous fangs, jolting in time with the pistons that were his legs. Closer, closer, closer, the dark gleaming eyes, the fangs, the inevitability of Fleabag's horrible death.

Fleabag whimpered, closed his eyes, prayed.

The killer bowler fired a cannonball of death. The air sizzled with hate and craziness and too many bad metaphors. Fleabag threw his bat up in front of his face, desperately fending off the red missile that would take his head off at the stump if it connected.

With Fleabag dead, the vampires would win by default.

The ball nicked the bat and sailed up in the air, a genuine Heavens-to-Betsy, lollypop catch.

No! No! After all the hard work, all the heartache, all the blood, sweat and tears . . . to lose in the final second.

Unlucky Chapter 13

Like most things in low-market books of gibberish like this (from the simplistic story summary on the back cover to the author's faked credentials on the front), the above chapter heading is bogus, spurious, erroneous and wrongus.

There's nothing unlucky in it at all . . .

The two vampire fielders raced for the ball, cracked heads, fell dead. The ball landed on the ground, rolling. Fleabag opened his eyes, amazed to find himself still alive.

'Run!' screamed Jason-Jock.

Fleabag stared down the pitch, saw his captain running and sprang out of his crease like a jumping-jack. Then he saw the kitten. It had wandered out of the crowd, meandered through the field looking for some attention and settled onto the pitch. Fleabag stopped dead in his tracks. He was petrified of kittens. Nothing could induce him to budge. His team screamed and howled from the benches. The vampire team hissed and spat and cursed from the sidelines.

Pandemonium reigned.

Screams and whistles. Shouts and incriminations. Threats of violence from parents. Unsavoury advice from old ladies.

It was deadset chaos.

Then, out of nowhere, Principal Skullwater streaked across the midnight pitch, his withered and wrinkled form as nude as the Creator created him. Bad form all round, from my observations, but I won't get in the way of time-honoured cricketing traditions like streaking, and certainly won't put myself in the way of a streaking Skullwater.

He skipped across the pitch, aged bits and wrinkles flying everywhere, collared the kitten in one swift move and popped it in a sack. 'Plump and young and juicy,' muttered Skullwater as he sprinted past on his naturalistic way. 'This kitten will do nicely for my dinner.'

Then the naked principal was gone, vanished into the darkness. So had the kitten.

And Fleabag ran, ran like the devil was on his tail. The vampire fieldsman pegged the ball from the outfield, straight at the wickets. The stumps tore apart like the little pigs' house of sticks just as Fleabag crossed the crease.

But Fleabag was safe. He'd made it.

The werewolves had won the Cup.

The howls of joy! The yelps of delight! The baying for vampire blood! The capering of those delighted dogs as they jostled and snarled and rough-housed and rolled and scuffled and scrambled and snapped their teeth, before completing the whole victory ceremony with a big, deep sniff of each others' butts.

It's a werewolf thing . . .

Next Monday the truck from Death Valley High delivered the portable classroom. It was a sweet victory finale for Horror High, a fully swish scene. I was supposed to cut the ribbon at the opening ceremony, but the security guards wouldn't let me through.

The two flash portable classrooms now squatted side by side, housing all the overflow students, with their two portable toilets housing all the overflow from the students . . . the finer details of which we definitely don't need to examine here.

Principal Skullwater pranced about, grinning, gaping, slapping backs and praising the victorious werewolves. Now he was their best mate, their biggest supporter, head of their fan club, the one and only person who'd believed in them from the very start, and never doubted they'd do it.

The shonky sod.

He'd checked the new portable classroom out, made sure everything was in its place and now proceeded around the rear to check the attached toilet block. This was the best part of all. These two extra dunnies would ease the chronic lunchtime toilet gridlock, discourage all those monsters ducking behind bushes and banish those interminable lines of straining students waiting for the can, man.

Oh yes, this was the highlight of winning the bet for Skullwater. He had a weird fixation with toilets and considered himself an expert in all things septic.

He sure wasn't an expert in etiquette. As far as good manners were concerned, Skullwater might just as well have been raised by wild lowland gorillas. He didn't bother to knock on the portable classroom's toilet door, just barged straight in. Perched on the throne was WG Grace, pants around his ankles, going about his business 19th-century style and reading a cricket magazine.

It might have been WG's quick temper or it might have been that powerful and recurring gypsy curse – nobody who witnessed it could say for sure – but the final effect was there for all to see.

The new classrooms may have looked impressive, but the truly notable fixture was the toilet block and its bold, post-modernist approach to interior design – Principal Skullwater stuffed headfirst down the bog!

THE END

About the Author

Paul Stafford is a literary consultant working in schools across Australia, and the author of nine books of teenage fiction. He grew up in Kurrajong Heights and now lives outside Bathurst, NSW. He studied print journalism at Mitchell CAE, graduating in 1989, but renounced the make-believe world of journalism for the hard and gritty reality of teenage fiction. Although a career in writing has meant abandoning his childhood dreams of wealth and respectability, he now gets to sleep late, dress scruffy and gnaw on the skulls of his enemies. It's a trade-off he's learnt to live with.

Acknowledgements

This book is dedicated to my darling wife Catarina. Without her nothing matters.

I'd like to acknowledge the fantastic support of my parents and family, Suzanne Bennett of the State Library of NSW, and Catherine McLelland of Lateral Learning.

These stories were really written to irritate my nephews and niece – Paddy Rutherford, Sam & Annika Clayton, and Kieran Stodart. As rotten kids go, they're not too bad, even if they smell that way.

A Sneak Preview of

The trouble started (as it often does in dozy, ozone-depleting stories like this) with a cheapo mail-order catalogue, an April Fool's Day prank gone wrong, and an over-protective father who refused to allow his son a pocketknife, pocket money or even a pocket.

It was Saturday morning in the Grim-Reaper household, and Mr Grim-Reaper was embroiled in an argument with his son, Nathan.

It wasn't that old man G-R wanted an argument. Au contraire, he just wished to relax over morning coffee and the weekend edition of the *Tombstone Times* – the quality newspaper for the well-read undead – but Nathan was on the bug again. Lately it seemed he was constantly on the bug about something.

This time Nathan reckoned he needed pocket money.

'I feed you, clothe you and pay your school fees; what do you want pocket money for?' Mr Grim-Reaper hissed irritably, in a voice reminiscent of the Ringwraiths from *Lord of the Rings*.

Boy, was he sick of comparisons to *that* film. Everyone he met these days, first thing they'd say after he'd introduced himself, "*You sound just like those spooky Ringwraiths from the Rings Trilogy.*" He couldn't wait to get his death grip on that fatso Kiwi film director and feed him and his Oscar to an orc.

'What do you want pocket money for?' Mr G-R repeated, sounding now like a car radiator boiling over.

'I want to buy a pocketknife,' replied Nathan, as reasonably as he could manage. Always attempt to reason with your recalcitrant parent, the *Undead Teenagers' Handbook* advised; adults pride themselves on being reasonable, so try to act like an adult.

'What do you want with a pocketknife?' Mr Grim-Reaper hissed. 'You don't even have a pocket.'

'Well I *would* have a pocket if you let me wear jeans like all the other kids at school,' reasoned Nathan.

'Seven hundred generations of Grim Reapers have worn menacing black robes,' growled father G-R, 'so why should you be any different?'

He took a sip of his coffee. It was cold.

'Yeah,' agreed Nathan, 'and seven hundred generations have carried a scythe. I wouldn't need a pocketknife if you let me carry a scythe. Why should I be the first not to have one?'

'I've told you a hundred times – you're too young. You'll get one when you're older. Scythes are dangerous. You'll cut yourself, or take somebody's head off, next thing you've got a lawsuit on your hands. First you prove yourself responsible, then you get a trainer scythe.'

A trainer scythe was made of rubber, and the equivalent of trainer wheels on a bicycle – baby stuff. Nathan frowned appropriately in response.

'Then in the meantime let me have a pocketknife,' Nathan begged.

'But you don't have a pocket.'

And so on . . .

Nathan was notoriously argumentative, his father was worse, and if you know anything about Grim Reapers and arguments you'll know they're like a dog with a bone: they just won't let it go. And you know how the saying goes – lay down with dogs, get up with fleas, start chasing cats . . .

All of which is totally irrelevant and beside the point.

The point was this: Nathan was chafing under his father's over-protectiveness. His dad wouldn't let him do *anything*. Wouldn't let him take any risks. Wouldn't let him act like a normal teenager.

Same old story.

Nathan tried telling his dad straight but the silly old geezer didn't get it; he'd just turned 50,000 years old and his teenage years were way too far gone for memory. Nathan consulted his teenage advice book, which was also useless; it suggested proving you were responsible through responsible behaviour, and demonstrating reasonableness by acting reasonably.

Big help. Thanks a bunch.

Nathan even resorted to watching *Finding Nemo* on DVD with his dad, pointing out how Nemo's over-protective father was just like Nathan's over-protective father. But Nathan's over-protective father didn't get the message at all, cried at the soppy bits, got scared at the scaredy bits, scarfed all the M&Ms and raved about how clever the animators were: 'Those images look so lifelike . . . *they* should've got the Oscar, not that fat *Lord of the Rings* swindler.'

It was useless. Nathan had to do something or he'd go completely bonkers.

Something had to change; he needed some freedom, some independence, some control over his life, and soon.

And then, when all hope seemed lost, Nathan was thrown a lifeline from a most unexpected source – Parent-Teacher Night at Horror High . . .